To my sisters Chris, Lynn, and Karen.

Carla Carlita Okidoki Octopus

Requests for permission to make copies of any part of the work should be submitted online at info@mascotbooks.com or mailed to Mascot Books, 560 Herndon Parkway #120, Herndon, VA 20170.

PRT0414A

Printed in the United States

ISBN-13: 9781620865675
ISBN-10: 162086567X

www.mascotbooks.com

Carla Carlita
Okidoki Octopus

Nicole Rondeau

Illustrated by
Ron Florendo

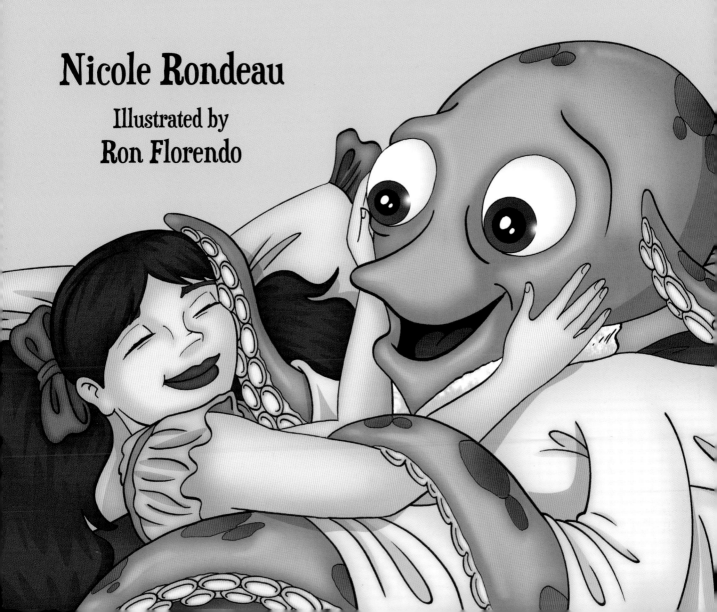

It was so hot outside. Carla Carlita thought she was going to melt. "Can we please, please, please go to the beach today?" she asked her parents. "I'm going to melt completely if we stay home. I'm going to be a people puddle!"

"No such thing as a people puddle," said her dad. "You won't melt."

"Please, please, PLEASE take me to the beach today!" begged Carla.

Her mom and dad looked at each other. "Okidoki," said her dad.

"THANK YOU!" shouted Carla. "That's awesome!"

Carla ran upstairs and packed her swimsuit, sunscreen, and beach toys. When she put on her sunglasses, she was ready to roll!

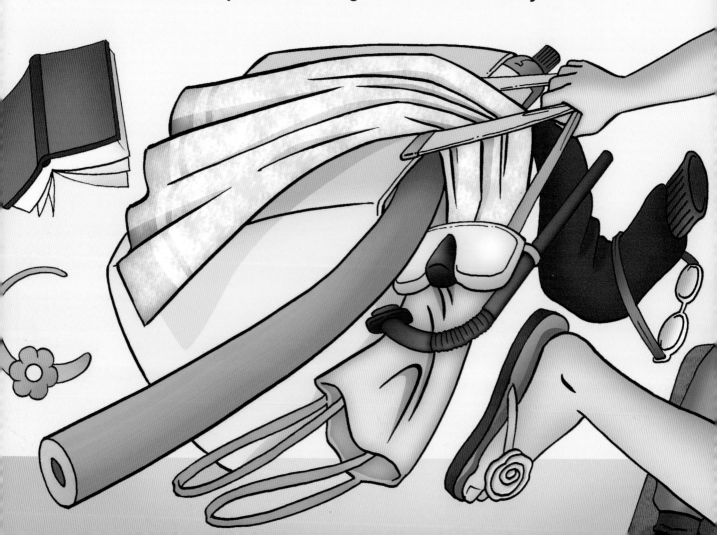

When they got to the beach, Carla ran as fast as she could into the water. It felt so cool! She sat in the water, squished the sand between her toes, and she flopped and jumped around. It felt great!

"Come and get a snack!" shouted her dad.

Carla ran out of the water and everyone on the beach screamed!

Their eyes bulged out of their heads, their hairs stood straight up, and they kept on screaming! "What's going on?" asked Carla. She was looking around but didn't see anything scary...until she looked down.

"ARGH!" screamed Carla. "THERE'S AN OCTOPUS ON ME!
THERE'S AN OCTOPUS ON ME!"

She jumped and shook and jumped and shook! She tried to shake it off, but nothing happened. He had his tentacles wrapped around her waist and he wouldn't let go.

Her dad grabbed a tentacle and yanked and pulled, but the octopus grabbed her dad's arm, juggled him in the air, and tossed him into the water. Everyone laughed and clapped. That was quite a show!

"That's so funny," said Carla. "Can I keep him?"

"It doesn't look like we have much choice. We can't get him off of you," said her mom.

"Okidoki," said her dad.

"That's a great name for him!" said Carla. "Okidoki Octopus!"

That night, Carla dressed him up in one of her nightgowns. He was actually pretty cute. When he snuggled up to Carla, she noticed Okidoki was very soft and squishy. Like Jell-O.

The next morning, Carla came down for breakfast and sat down at the table. "What's for breakfast?" she asked.

"Cereal," said her mother.

"What's Okidoki going to eat?" asked Carla.

"Maybe fish," said her dad. He opened a can of sardines and tried to give it to Okidoki. Six of his tentacles picked up six fish and threw them every which way!

"I don't think he likes fish," said Carla.

Okidoki grabbed the box of Loopy Fruity Loops, stuck his tentacles in the box, tossed the cereal in the air, and ate every piece. Okidoki loved it!

Later that day, Carla's friend Liam called. "Hey, Carla," he said. "Do you want to come over to ride my horse today?" he asked.

"Of course!" she said. She loved going over to his place to ride horses. She put on her cowboy boots and hat, and Okidoki wore a cowboy hat and eight cowboy boots.

Off they went!

Once they got to Liam's, Carla and Okidoki climbed onto their horse. Okidoki held the reins and ate cereal at the same time. He was on his fifth box! When they passed under a big tree, Okidoki swung his tentacle up and grabbed onto a branch. The horse kept running while Carla and Okidoki were left hanging from the tree!

"HELP! HELP!" shouted Carla.

Liam's dad came running. He put up a ladder and carried them both down. That was scary!

The next day, Carla and Okidoki went to school. Everyone surrounded Carla. They couldn't believe their eyes! One boy tried to touch Okidoki, but he grabbed his hat and ate it!

Carla had a math test that morning. While she was busy answering questions, she heard someone shout.

"Wow! Look at Josie's hair!" screamed the girl in the next row.

"Oh wow!" shouted the kids in the class. Okidoki had used six of his tentacles to braid Josie's hair! There were hundreds of braids everywhere! Kids started lining up for Okidoki to braid their hair, even the boys and, of course, Carla.

At recess, everyone went outside to play. It was a gorgeous day! Carla and her friends were using sidewalk chalk to draw pictures on the cement play pad. They drew dinosaurs, dragons, and monkeys. All of a sudden, Okidoki pointed seven tentacles towards the school wall and shot out ink everywhere! His tentacles were all over the place, and the ink was flying here, there, and everywhere.

When Okidoki was done, the entire schoolyard was silent. Then all of the children and teachers started to clap and cheer. Okidoki had drawn a beautiful picture of the ocean filled with whales, dolphins, octopi, and hundreds of fish. It was truly magical! Okidoki was smiling as much as an octopus could smile.

"Look," said Carla. "I think that's Okidoki's mom and dad." There was a drawing of two big octopi hugging.

Carla felt a little sad. Maybe Okidoki missed his mom and dad.

The next day, Carla and her mom went grocery shopping. Her mother parked the car, and they started walking towards the store. Suddenly they heard crying from up above.

They looked up and saw a small child dangling from a balcony.

"Oh my goodness!" shouted her mother.

"Mommy, that baby's going to fall!" screamed Carla.

Okidoki jumped onto the wall and, using his suction cups, started climbing up the building while still holding Carla!

Okidoki grabbed the child with one long tentacle, then started zipping down the building. When they got to the bottom, a huge crowd had gathered and everyone was cheering and shouting his name. "OKIDOKI! OKIDOKI!"

A fireman took hold of the little boy and said, "Thanks for being a hero and saving this little child." The crowd went wild!

"I'm going to take you two to the beach. We're going to celebrate!" said her mother while handing Carla her jacket.

"Yay!" shouted Carla. She started spinning around in circles. Okidoki was spinning with her and started to turn green!

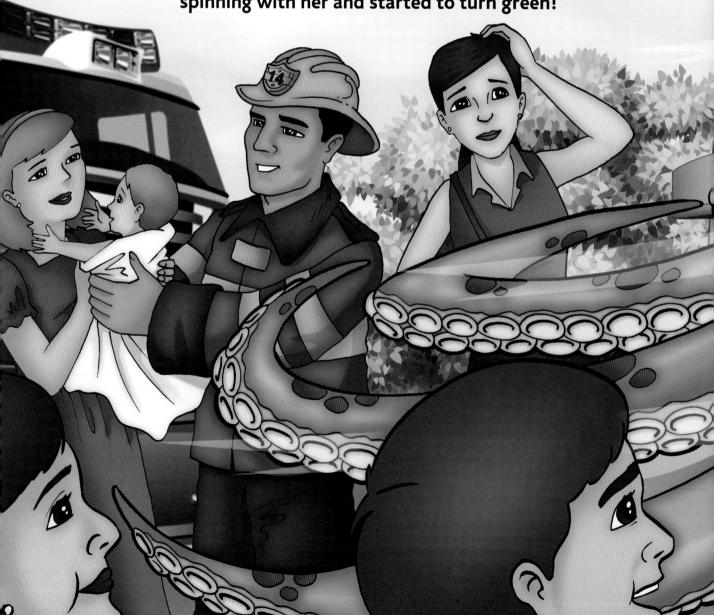

When they got to the beach, Carla ran into the water and started splashing water everywhere. When she finally came out to dry herself, her mom was staring at her.

"Carla, where's Okidoki?" she asked.

Carla looked down, behind, around, everywhere. No octopus. She ran back into the water. Nothing. She couldn't believe it. Okidoki was gone.

Her mother hugged her. "It's all right, Carla. He's back where he belongs," she said.

They both looked back at the water. Okidoki popped out of the water and was sitting on a rock. Then the rock started to get bigger and bigger, and came right out of the water. It was his mother! They waved then swam off.

"I'm sure happy Okidoki's with his mother," said Carla. "That's the best thing in the world, but I am going to miss him terribly."

Then she gave her mother a super big hug.

Photo courtesy of Alicia Drinkwalter

Nicole lives in Brandon, Manitoba, with her husband and four children. She began storytelling as a child, entertaining her siblings and cousins at a young age. She started writing when her children were small, drawing from their hilarious antics; they are her inspiration, and continue to be. She enjoys their laughter and loves to dote on her grandchild. Because of her husband's career, they spent many years moving throughout the country. Today she has a very successful business relocating seniors and also working for a major newspaper.